LITTLE SIMON

An imprint of Simon & Schuster Children's Publishing Division
1230 Avenue of the Americas, New York, New York 10020
First Little Simon hardcover edition July 2015
Copyright © 2015 by Ramon Olivera. All rights reserved,
including the right of reproduction in whole or in part in any form.
LITTLE SIMON is a registered trademark of Simon & Schuster, Inc.,
and associated colophon is a trademark of Simon & Schuster, Inc.
For information about special discounts for bulk purchases,
please contact Simon & Schuster Special Sales at
1-866-506-1949 or business@simonandschuster.com.
The Simon & Schuster Speakers Bureau can bring authors to
your live event. For more information or to book an event
contact the Simon & Schuster Speakers Bureau at
1-866-248-3049 or visit our website at www.simonspeakers.com.
Manufactured in China 0515 SCP
2 4 6 8 10 9 7 5 3 1
ISBN 978-1-4814-3242-9 (hc)
ISBN 978-1-4814-3243-6 (eBook)

For Joyce,
Sophia,
and Alex

ABCs on Wings

RAMON OLIVERA

LITTLE SIMON

NEW YORK LONDON TORONTO SYDNEY NEW DELHI

 **Aa** is for **ace.**

Bb is for biplane.

Cc is for carrier.

Dd is for deck.

Ee is for engines.

Ff is for fuel.

Gg is for glider.

Hh is for helicopter.

Ii is for intake.

Jj is for jet.

Kk is for *Kitty Hawk.*

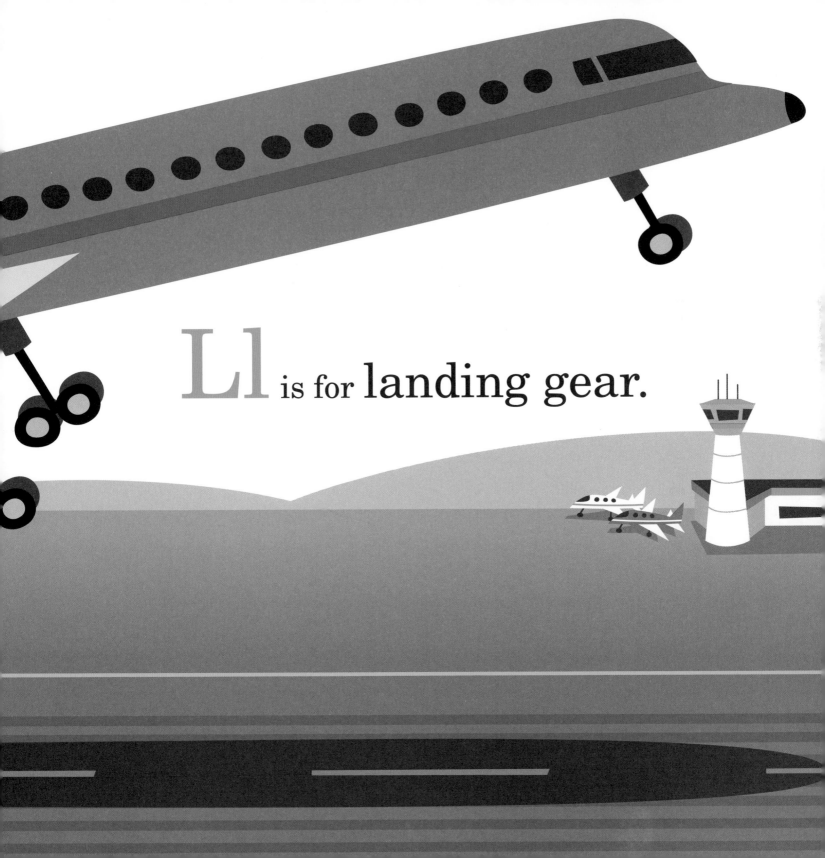

Ll is for landing gear.

Mm
is for map.

Nn
is for navigator.

Oo is for oxygen.

Pp is for pilot.

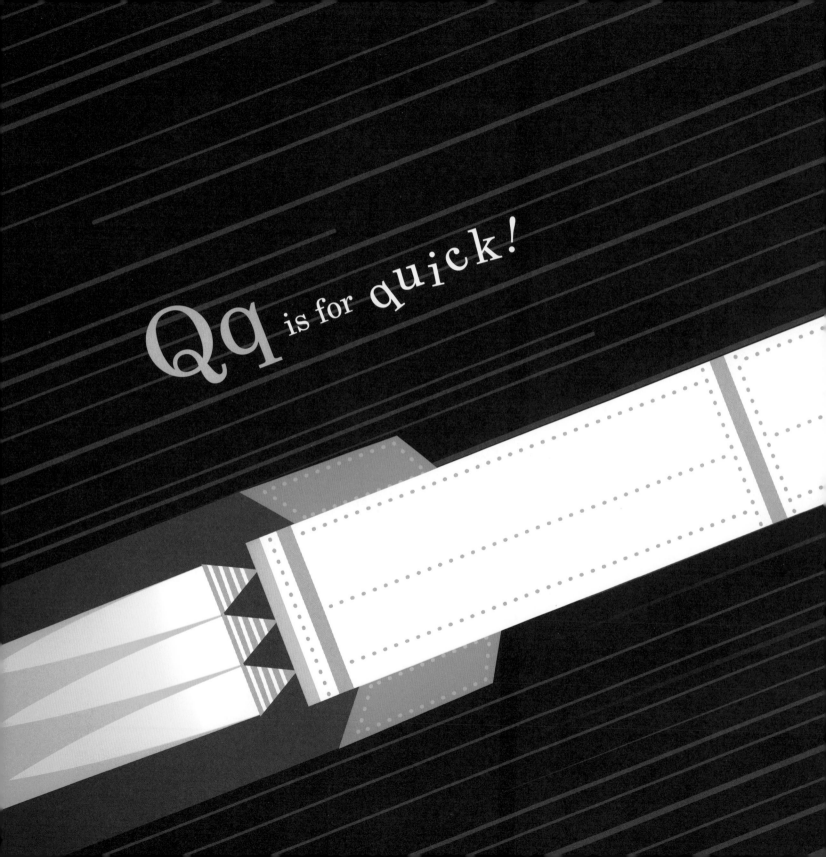

Qq is for quick!

Rr is for rocket.

Ss is for **space capsule.**

Tt is for turbulence…

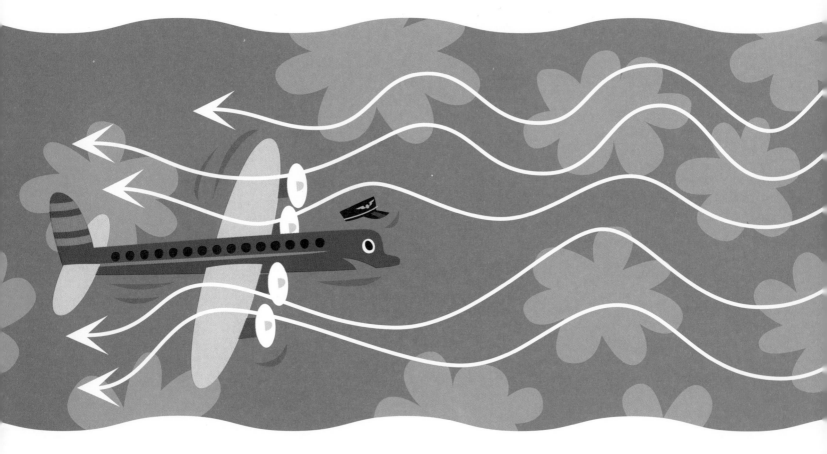

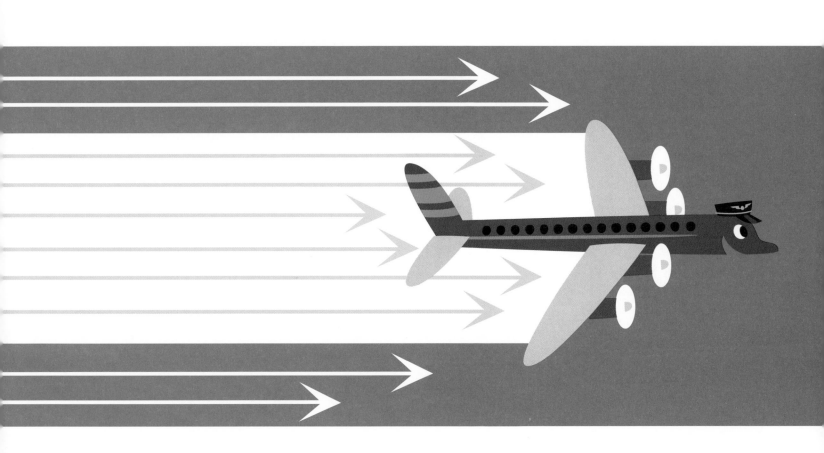

and **tailwind.**

Uu is for U.F.O.

Vv is for vanished.

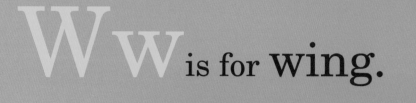

Ww is for wing.

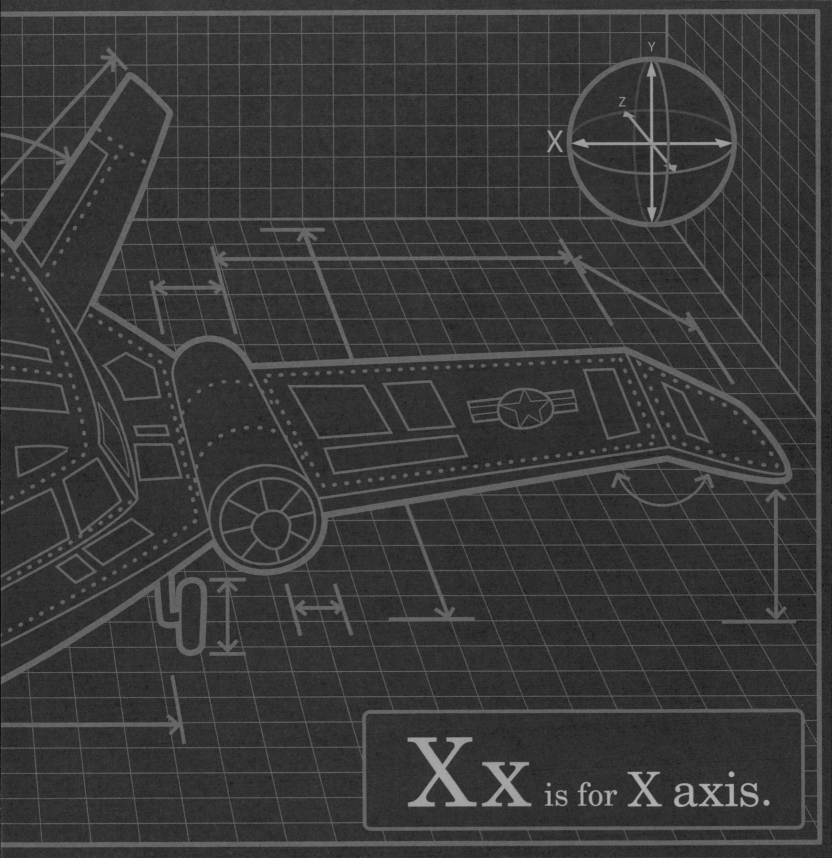

Xx is for **X** axis.

Yy is for yay! yahoo! yippee!

Zz is for zeppelin.